A. Clark Tuttle

Descriptive catalogue of adapted fruit trees

Small fruits, plants, etc.

A. Clark Tuttle

Descriptive catalogue of adapted fruit trees
Small fruits, plants, etc.

ISBN/EAN: 9783741198922

Manufactured in Europe, USA, Canada, Australia, Japa

Cover: Foto ©Andreas Hilbeck / pixelio.de

Manufactured and distributed by brebook publishing software
(www.brebook.com)

A. Clark Tuttle

Descriptive catalogue of adapted fruit trees

⚬DIRECTIONS, ÷ TERMS, ÷ ETC.⚬

PLEASE order early, before any varieties are exhausted and you will then get what you want. If you leave the selection of varieties to me I will use my best judgment in the choice. Tell me what your soil is; the location as to elevation, slope, protection, etc. Also state your troubles in growing fruit and I will aid you all I can.

Please write your name plainly, giving the post office, express office, county and state. Also the name of the railway. Enclose the amount of the bill, and I will do my best to sent you. If any claim is made it should be sent inside ten days, to receive attention. We deliver all packages to the forwarders free, and then our control ceases and of course our responsibility also. Look to the forwarders for all damages occurring en route. Packing is done in the best possible manner. We make it a point to pack as light as possible and at the same time insure the best condition of the stock. All goods are packed free and everything tied and labeled distinctly.

Mistakes sometimes occur. We warrant our stock to be true to name with the express understanding that if any proves untrue, we will replace it with other, but in no case will we be liable for damages.

This is a stationary institution and can be found. Its guarantee is worth something. Its reputation for furnishing "pedigree" stock adapted to the North-west cost toil and expense and is to be maintained. When we sell short we do not order Alabama stock to fill orders. Try us.

Remit by postoffice money order on Baraboo, express money order, registered letter or draft, but no postage stamps postal notes or private checks. Address all letters to

A. CLARK TUTTLE,
Baraboo, Wis.

INTRODUCTORY.

IN this day of the world it is said to be nearly impossible to sell anything except by personal solicitation. The wholesale grocer of the larger cities has commercial solicitors traveling from one customer to another. The tree-grower must send out his agents to solicit the trade, or his competitor will get it. It has become almost impossible to get any mail orders. Do the people get any better goods? Do they find the prices better? Is the peddler any more reliable than the nurseryman? Is there any advantage gained by giving the orders to the first smooth-tongued traveler, instead of mailing it to the nearest nurseryman noted for honest deal and honest goods? I employ no agents or traveling men, but am obliged to wholesale to those who sell direct to the planter. I would much prefer to receive the orders from the planter, and he would be the gainer EVERY TIME. I know of parties within two miles of this nursery, who have bought bills of trees several times of irresponsible traveling treemen, and they probably will again. They pay three times the prices that live trees of the same varieties would cost at this nursery, and they have the vacant orchard rows to show for the ducats expended. They are the people who are so loud in denouncing Wisconsin as totally incapable of producing fruit, now and forever. This catalogue is not for that class of persons. It is for those who would like to raise fruit, and buy intending to do their part towards making their purchases a success; who take a live, progressive, instructive, high-toned horticultural journal like the "Popular Gardening" of Buffalo, N. Y., and read it and profit by its reliable teachings. We hope to prove to these parties that OUR STOCK IS RELIABLE. That our advice as to what is best to plant is valuable. That our way of doing business is not only pleasant but profitable to our customers. To our old customers we are grateful, and to the new ones, we will promise the strictest attention to their wants, hoping to add all their names to our long list of kind friends who buy of us because they have found it paid them to do so. TRY US with a small order.

On receipt of your trees if they appear to be dry, bury them TOPS AND ALL, in moist earth for a few days. If it has been freezing weather and you have reason to think there is frost in them, put the package, UNOPENED, into a dark cellar, for a day or two, and let the frost come out gradually, and if the roots were well mossed in packing, they will be uninjured. When Strawberries are received and you are not quite ready to plant them, be sure that the roots are kept moist, without moistening the foliage, and put them on the cellar bottom. Evergreens *must be kept from drying the roots in the least.* Heel them in as fast as unpacked and not allow the sun or wind to reach the bare roots for a moment. A good way is to prepare a clay puddle and immerse the roots, which will give them a coating that will exclude sun and air. Then heel them in. After the sap of an evergreen once hardens it never flows again. The tree is dead, though the foliage may not show it for many days.

BURYING TREES.

SELECT a spot where the water does not stand. Dig an open trench long enough to take the trees laid singly, side by side, with roots in the trench and tops along the ground, at right angles with the trench. Cut Roman numerals in the back of the labels, and mark the same against the name in your book record, as the moist earth will take out the pencil marks. Then open each variety and place them, driving a stake between each variety. After all are in, throw fine earth, free from all rubbish, among and on the roots, shaking and tramping enough to fill all interstices among the roots. Cover roots one foot and slant off to the tops, covering the extreme tops about three inches. Put no straw or other rubbish on or near them to attract mice. In the Spring open carefully with a fork, not to gall the trunks or break the branches, and plant *as soon as the frost is out sufficiently.*

COLLECTIONS.

THE following collections will be selected from the best stock, and will be nicely packed in moss and burlaps, each variety being tied separately and labeled. We make no changes in the contents of any package. Please order by the numbers. Any three $1.00 collections for $2.50. Any two $3 00 collections for $5.00:

No. 1.	1 Transparent Apple, 4 to 6 feet	30
	1 Switzer " "	30
	1 Zolotoref " "	30
	1 Longfield " "	30
		$1.20
No. 2.	1 Anis " "	30
	1 Hibernal " "	30
	1 Lord's " "	30
	1 Repka Malenka Apple "	30
		$1.20
No. 3.	1 Blackwood Apple '	35
	1 Vargul " "	40
	1 Antonovka " "	50
		$1.25
No. 4.	1 Whitney No. 20 Crab "	25
	1 Ostheim Cherry '	50
	1 DeSoto Plum "	50
		$1.25
No. 5.	1 Early Victor Grape	50
	1 Moore's Early Grape	50
	1 Concord Grape	25
		$1.25
No. 6.	1 Moore's Early Grape	50
	1 Worden Grape	30
	1 Brighton Grape	40
		$1.20
No. 7.	1 Early Victor Grape	50
	1 Empire State Grape	75
		$1.25

No. 8. 2 Fay Currant 50
        2 White Grape Currant 12
        2 Victoria Currant . ...,........ 12
        2 Cherry Currant 12
        2 La Versailes Currant 12
        2 Lee's Prolific Currant 25

                                            $1,23

No. 9. 3 Downing Gooseberry.... ......,......... . 60
        3 Smith's Improved Gooseberry.......... ... 70

                                            $1.30

No. 10. 5 Lucretia Dewberry 40
        10 Ancient Briton Blackberry 30
        10 Stone's Hardy   "   30
        10 Snyder   "   30

                                            $1 30

No. 11. 5 Hilborn (Black Cap) Raspberry   30
        10 Tyler (Black Cap) Raspberry 25
        10 Ohio (Black Cap) Raspberry... 25
        10 Turner Raspberry 25
        10 Cuthbert Raspberry....................... 25

                                            $1.30

No. 12, 10 Jessie Strawberry....... . ...'....... 40
        10 Bubach No. 5, Strawberry.............. 30
        10 Warfield No. 2, Strawberry,................. 40
        10 Wilson (Pure)................................ . 20

                                            $1.30

Any of the foregoing numbers for $1.00. Any of the following numbers for $3.00:

No. 1. 12 New Russian Apple Trees, 4 to 6 feet, of our
        selection of 4 sorts $3.60

No. 2. 6 New Russian Apple 4 to 6 feet........... .... 1.80
        2 English Morello Cherry .. .. , ... 60
        1 Wragg Cherry   .... ,.............. 60
        2 Whitney No 20, Crab 50

                                            $3.50

No. 3. 2 Vargul Apples 4 to 6 feet..... 80
        2 Antonovka 4 to 6 feet   ... .········ 1.00
        2 DeSoto Plum, 4 to 6 feet 1.00
        1 Forest Garden Plum, 4 to 6 feet ... .,..... 50
        1 English Morello Cherry 30

                                            $3.60

No. 4.   2 Moore's Early Grape 1.00
         2 Worden   " 60
         2 Brighton   " 80
         2 Lady   " 1.00
         1 Concord   " 25

                                     $3.65

No. 5.   5 Fay Currant 1.25
         5 White Grape Currant 30
         6 Lucretia Dewberry 48
       10 Ancient Briton Blackberry................ 30
       10 Stone's Hardy   " 30
       10 Tyler Raspberry 25
         2 Downing Gooseberry...................... 40
         2 Smith's Improved Gooseberry............ 40

                                     $3.68

No. 6.   50 Jessie Strawberry 1.50
       50 Haverland Strawberry.................... 1.50
       25 Bubach No. 5 Strawberry................ 60

                                     $3.60

No. 7.   8 Norway Spruce 2½ feet, for $3.00
No. 8.   8 Balsam Fir, 3 feet, for $3.00
No. 9.   8 White Spruce, 2 feet, for 3.00
No. 10.   2 Norway Spruce, 2½ feet 1.00
         2 Balsam Fir, 3 feet 1.00
         2 White Spruce, 2 feet 75
         2 American Arbor Vitae, 2 feet 75

                                     $3.50

No. 12.   1 Pyramidalis Arbor Vitae 1.00
         1 Little Gem   "   " 1.00
         1 Mountain Pine 50
         1 Cut-leaved Weeping Birch 1.00

                                     $3.50

APPLES.

TWENTY-TWO years ago we obtained our first scions from Russia, and for more than fifteen years have had the new Russians in orchard. We planted at the same time an orchard of 300 Duchess. The per cent. of fruit in this orchard is ten times greater than in an orchard of 80 varieties of new Russians growing near it. The only trees killed by the winter of 1884-5, of the new Russians, are two Crimean apples and one that came to us as Green Transparent, which proved to be White Astrachan. Some eight or ten varieties have proved worthless by blight. Of the 300 Duchess 20 were killed outright by that winter, and many others more or less injured. In sending to Russia for scions, we hoped to get at least a dozen varieties as hardy as the Duchess, and fruit that would successfully compete in the markets with the old favorites of the East. The results of the tests we have made, abundantly prove that very many of the new Russians are hardier than the Duchess and equal in quality to any of the old American sorts, giving us fruit in season from *very early to very late*. The only thing in the way of the general planting of the new Russian fruits, is the loss of confidence in them occasioned by the dissemination by some Wisconsin and Minnesota nurserymen, of trees purporting to be Russians, which *were grown in Alabama*.

Before discarding the Russians we would ask the planters of Wisconsin to make a trial of, at least, a few of our trees. If you will leave the selection to us, we think we can furnish you trees that will succeed. Our stock is grown here. The scions are taken from the trees which have borne, and consequently *must be true to name.* Try a dozen.

TRANSPARENT—Mr. Lovett, of New Jersey, says: "It ripens fully ten days in advance of the Early Harvest, and the past season I picked fully ripe specimens on the 30th of June. Size medium; light transparent lemon yellow, smooth waxen surface; flesh melting, juicy and of excellent quality, and for an early apple, an exceptionally good keeper and shipper—surpassing far in these important points Early Harvest, Primate and other early varieties. Tree a free upright grower, very prolific and a remarkably early bearer, frequently producing in the nursery row, the second year from the bud.

YELLOW SWEET—Earlier than Transparent. Tree a fine grower and very hardy. Fruit yellow with reddish bronze on the sun side; flesh firm and agreeably sweet, good for dessert and cooking. Keeps well for so early an apple.

EARLY GLASS—Tree is extremely hardy and free from blight—never loses a bud from severity of climate—is a fine and regular grower and good bearer. Fruit self colored, with little color on sun side. Good bearer and keeps well if picked before over-ripe.

ENORMOUS—The largest of August apples. Some specimens have been grown here measuring 14 inches in circumference. Almost covered with deep red, it is very showy. Flesh a little coarse but a good sub-acid flavor. Season, August and September.

PROLIFIC SWEETING—A yellow apple of medium to large size. Dr. Hoskins says the "best of the sweet apples for market purposes." Tree, a very stocky grower and great bearer. Is hardy at St. Petersburg.

CHARLAMOFF—A very large yellow apple, mildly acid, ripens at the end of August. A good grower and productive. Season, September.

SWITZER—Tree very hardy, handsome, upright grower, and very productive. Fruit medium to large, entirely covered with red. Flesh white, fine-grained, tender, sub-acid, with a delightful quince-like flavor. An excellent keeper for its season, and one of the best fall apples. October.

VASILIS LARGEST—This belongs to the same family as Green Streaked, and Zolotoref, a little more color perhaps and tree a little more upright. October and November.

ARABIAN—As received from the department is of the Duchess type of apple, but a little better keeper. A remarkably free grower in the nursery, and makes a very symmetrical orchard tree. October.

BEAUTIFUL ARCADE—Tree an upright, pretty grower in the nursery, in the orchard more spreading. Very hardy. Fruit above medium size, delicately striped with pink on light green. Flesh white, tender, juicy, very pleasant sweet. Dessert and cooking. November.

GREEN STREAKED—A very large showy apple, striped with red, somewhat coarse in texture, but a salable apple, that keeps into winter. Distinct green veinings in the flesh are characteristic and probably suggested the name. Season, October to January.

GLASS GREEN—As received by me from the Department, is an improved Duchess. Is hardier and much better nursery grower, and the fruit is a milder acid and keeps till November.

RASPBERRY—A beautiful little bright red, dessert apple. A very pleasant, fresh and sprightly sub-acid, with a nice after taste. Flesh white with scarlet veins near the skin. Tree, upright and vigorous, and stands the worst winters at St. Petersburg without injury. Its beauty and fine flavor, and the perfect hardiness of the tree, will command favor wherever planted. October to January.

HEIDORNS STREAKED—A very beautiful large sized apple, dull red splashed on yellow, very sweet and of delicate texture. Dr. Regel, of St. Petersburg, says: It bears a large amount of fruit every year, and stands the climate of St. Petersburg. Please note that St. Petersburg is in 60 degrees north latitude, or 1,136 miles north of this place. Season, October to January.

YELLOW ARCADE—A yellow apple with a little red on the sun side. Flesh tender, juicy, slight sub-acid. Dessert and cooking. November.

GOLDEN WHITE—Fruit is medium to large, with no cavity. In color a dull green turning to yellow with some show of red striping on the sun side; basin bronzed and russeted. Flesh tender; flavor a mild acid. Tree rather slow in the nursery, but vigorous in the orchard, and a great and annual bearer. Buds very wooly and prominent. Season, November and December.

BARLOFF—Of the Alexander type as to size, shape and color. Flesh white and agreeably vinous-sweet. Is a nice grower and productive. Will undoubtedly become popular as an early winter sweet apple. Season, November and December.

ZOLOTOREFF—Undoubtedly the best of the large fall apples. A large, cylindrical, showy apple; deep red, with splashes of dark green in the basin. Flesh a little coarse, but juicy and spicy, with an agreeable after taste. Season, November to January.

LITTLE HAT—Dr. Regel says: "A globular fruit of full medium size. On the sunny side a pale blush with a good deal of dark red in stripes and splashes. Flesh greenish-white, juicy and a little sweet. A good looking fruit which ripens in September, and keeps through December. For house use only." Tree is a remarkably fine grower in the nursery, and perfectly hardy. November.

JUICY BURR—A very hardy tree and nice grower. Fruit resembles the Duchess in size, shape and color, but better quality and keeps through November.

WATERMELON—A very strong grower. Stands perfectly the climate of St. Petersburg. Fruit one of the largest; somewhat oblong in shape. Color yellow with light and dark crimson stripes.

Flesh greenish white, with an agreeable acid taste. A fine looking dessert and cooking apple. November.

RED ANIS--When Mr. Gibb questioned the people of Russia, as to which was the hardiest apple, they invariably replied: "Anis." Fruit a medium sized, flat apple. Color, dark carmine with some dingy yellow on the shady side. Flesh greenish white, juicy and sour. Keeps until January.

LONG ARCADE—A medium sized apple, much like Red Astrachan in form and color. Flesh, white and fine grained; flavor, a mild pleasant acid. Tree good grower and very hardy, bearing quite young. Season, December and January.

CZAR'S THORN—A sweet apple, oblong, of large size. Color, red on yellow. Tree is very hardy and a profuse bearer. December to January.

WHITE APPLE—Size medium. Greenish yellow, all one color. Flesh white, sub-acid, tender and juicy, with an agreeable, vinous acid flavor. Good for kitchen and dessert. Tree endures, uninjured, the worst winters of St. Petersburg. December to January.

SKROUT GERMAN—A very pretty, regular grower in the nursery and forms a beautiful orchard tree. Very productive and does not blight much. Fruit above medium, regular in shape, pale yellow with considerable red on the sun-side, and light and dark carmine stripes. Flesh is fine grained, tender and juicy, an agreeable, vinous acid. One of the best for dessert and kitchen. January.

ZUSOFF—Tree a fine, upright grower in the nursery and more spreading in the orchard. Very productive. Fruit medium, bright red. hangs well on the tree. Flesh crisp, juicy pleasant sub-acid. Fine for dessert, showy on the table. Good shipper. January.

KOURSK'S ANIS—One of the best of the Anis family. Tree a good grower and very hardy. Fruit above medium in size and keeps through January. Flesh yellowish white, pleasant acid. Good dessert apple.

LONGFIELD—An early winter apple of fine quality and very attractive in appearance, having a bright carmine cheek, gradually fading into the most beautiful peach blush, and then into a delicate waxen lemon color. A fine basket fruit. Dr. Regel says: "Neither the cold, nor the winds, nor the storms of the intensely Steppe climate of Serepta, have disturbed the growth of this tree. Of 100 different varieties growing in the garden of Mr. Langerfield—from whom the name—only this one bears fruit every year." It is a prodigious and very regular bearer, is a somewhat irregular grower in the nursery, but soon becomes a shapely tree in the orchard. Season January.

WHITE PIGEON—An extra hardy tree and good bearer. Fruit medium size, conic in form with wrinkled eye and no basin. Sweet, with peculiar but pleasant flavor, tender and juicy. January and February.

HIBERNAL—A valuable early winter variety, large and showy, light yellow, striped and blotched with red. Quite acid and very good for cooking. Tree hardy and superb grower. Season January and February.

BLACKWOOD—A favorite winter dessert apple on the Volga and commands an extra price on account of its fine quality. Medium size, greenish yellow with a little red. Flesh white, tender, juicy, agreeably vinous acid, with a very pleasant aftertaste. A good dessert and kitchen apple which keeps through February.

BORSOORFER—Is an apple of German origin about as hardy as the Wealthy, but of such fine quality as to warrant a trial in favorable locations. Ask a German about the Borsdorfer and he will tell you "It is the best apple that ever was." Fruit below medium in size, form and color resembles Ben Davis, flesh firm and of fine texture, sub-acid, rich and very good. Keeps through the winter.

RED QUEEN—Good grower and very hardy. Fruit medium to large, dark green with dull red on the sunside. Good shipping. March.

VARGUL—One of the most popular apples in Russia. When mature is a light yellow, with a reddish brown on the sunside, covering one-third the apple. Is large, to quite large and ribbed. Flesh yellowish white, soft, juicy, rich sub-acid and very nice after taste. Its fine size and excellent flavor recommends it among the best. Is extremely hardy and as yet no blight. March.

LORD'S APPLE—This is one of the best of the new Russians we have tested. Tree hardy and fine grower. Fruit large; shape, size, color and bloom resembles the Blue Pearmain and keeps as well. A clear, strong but pleasant acid, hangs well on the tree and bears abundantly. Stands the most trying winters of St. Petersburg. March and April.

REPKA MALENKA—One of the valuable new Russian apples from its keeping qualities, as it has kept till the June of the second year, with ordinary care. Mr. Webster, of Vermont, says, "It is an enormous biennial bearer. It is too hard to eat until warm weather in the spring, when it gradually ripens and becomes tender. spicy and of good quality and flavor." Mr. Sias says of it at winter meeting of Minnesota Horticultural Society, in Feb., 1886: "It was the best keeper shown. It tasted fresh and tart as if fresh picked from the tree." March and onward.

ANTONOVKA—This is the "King apple of the Russian steppes." Dr. Regel says, "This is one of the most highly prized and widely grown apples in Russia. It grows in the northern part of the Province of St. Petersburg, at Valaam, along the Baltic Sea and in eastern Russia. It is subacid, with an agreeable after taste; firm and juicy. It keeps till July, and is a delicate dessert fruit. This tree grows so readily in the far North, and has such a combination of good points, that many grow scarcely anything else. It is very much liked by the people, and brings the highest prices."

Beside the foregoing new Russian apples, we have the

WEALTHY—Minnesota's well known seedling. Fruit medium to large, oblate, skin very smooth, whitish yellow, shaded with deep red in the sun, and spotted in the shade. Flesh white, firm, tender, juicy, lively sub-acid; very good. December to February.

DUCHESS OF OLDENBURG—So well known as to need no description. It is still the fruit from which points of hardiness are graded in the north-west.

ORANGE WINTER—An apple which originated in this county. The original tree has now stood in quite sandy soil since 1850 and is perfectly healthy, bearing regular crops of fruit alternate years. Fruit is above medium in size, a light green and yellow, with red on one side. Flesh is yellowish white, rich, fine-grained, pleasant sub-acid and keeps through the winter.

WHITNEY (No. 20) **CRAB**—The best of all the crab apples, but should be gathered as soon as the seeds are black. The finest grower in the nursery, and makes a very symmetrical orchard tree. Great and regular bearer. Fruit three times the size of Transcendent; carmine with darker stripes. Nice fruit to eat from the tree.

CHERRIES.

OSTHEIM--A new variety which is very generally raised in Russia and endures the climate of Vladimir. It is above medium in size, sweet and rich, a good bearer and perfectly healthy. 4 to 6 feet, well branched.

WRAGG—Is a valuable seedling originated in Iowa. It is proving to be valuable for the north-west, as it is hardy and healthy; bears well. Fruit good size and pleasant as a dessert fruit.

English Morello, Early Richmond and Late Kentish are old sorts well known.

PLUMS

DE SOTO—Originated in Wisconsin, of native blood. Is very hardy, healthy and productive. Fruit nearly as large as the Lombard, freestone, solid fleshed, rich and sweet.

FOREST GARDEN--Ripens a little in advance of the De Soto, which it closely resembles in tree and is as hardy and healthy. Fruit something like the Yellow Egg in appearance.

WOLF—Originated in Iowa and is one of the best for the north-west. It is a dark red, solid fleshed fruit, and great bearer.

Also the **MINER**, which is proving valuable where of sufficient age, as it does not bear young.

GRAPES.

EARLY VICTOR—Season of the Janesville but much better fruit. Black. Bunch and berry medium, cluster compact. Tender, sweet, rich and very good.

MOORE'S EARLY—Two weeks earlier than the Concord. Should be in every collection.

BRIGHTON—Dark red. One of the most desirable of the new grapes. Ripens with the Worden.

EMPIRE STATE—A very strong grower. Best of the white grapes. Earlier than Concord. Keeps well.

LADY—A very choice white grape. Healthy but not as vigorous as the Empire State. Fruit nice size and very fine quality.

WORDEN—Black. Bunch and berry large. Quality much better than Concord and a week earlier. For home use it is one of the very best of the blacks.

CURRANTS.

Currants require the best of cultivation and high feed. The fence corner theory of old times, is—we are glad to say—discarded. The worms have weeded out the shiftless and careless growers, and the enterprising ones soon found it paid to feed and cultivate this wholesome fruit.

Plant your currants in rows six feet apart, and three feet in the row, keep clean from weeds, and top dress occasionally with rotten manure, and when the worms appear, dust the foliage thoroughly with powdered White Hellebore while the dew is on, repeating it after three days. This if attended to promptly, will exterminate the last worm.

FAY'S PROLIFIC—This is truly a great advance in currants. It is all the most enthusiastic claim for it. Equals the cherry in size of berry, in bunch twice the size, better in flavor, with much less acid, and five times as productive and from its peculiar stem, is less expensive to pick. The cherry currant has been sold very generally for the Fay's, and it has damaged its character. I get my stock direct from the introducer at Fredonia, N. Y., and *know it is true.*

WHITE GRAPE — The best white currant. Bunches large and long, berry large and of the best quality, being less acid than others. Prolific and strong grower.

VICTORIA—A valuable variety, ripening as it does after all others are gone. Bunches very long, berry of medium size, brilliant red and of excellent quality. Bushes good growers and profuse bearers. No collection should be without it.

IMPROVED RED DUTCH—Is a great improvement over the well known Red Dutch, in size of berry and bunch.

LEE'S PROLIFIC—A black variety of recent introduction and one that marks a great advance in the Blacks. It is earlier than the Naples, with very large berries, longer and larger clusters, and even more prolific than that productive variety.

BERRIES.

GOOSEBERRIES.

DOWNING—Fruit larger than Houghton; nice, upright, stocky grower, almost entirely free from mildew. Roundish, light green, with distinct veins; skin smooth, flesh rather soft, juicy and very good.

SMITH'S IMPROVED—From Vermont. Large, oval, light green, with bloom; flesh moderately firm, sweet and good. Vigorous grower.

BLACKBERRIES.

One of the most profitable fruits to grow for market. Plant in rows eight feet apart and three feet in the row. Give the best of cultivation and high feed. Pinch back all new canes when they reach 18 inches and the arms at 12 inches. Keep the crop as near the ground as possible. Treat all sprouts as weeds. Cover in the winter, after bearing down the canes carefully and putting on a spade or two of earth to hold them down, with evergreen boughs or corn stalks.

SNYDER—Is too well known to need a description, but is the earliest of the trio, viz: Snyder, Ancient Briton and Stone's Hardy.

ANCIENT BRITON—Is probably the most profitable blackberry grown. In quality, is first-class. Productiveness not excelled if equalled. Should plant three-fourths of this variety, one-eighth Snyder for early and one-eighth Stone's Hardy for late.

STONE'S HARDY — Keeps up well the character of its predecessor in the season. The drupes are not quite as large as those in the Ancient Briton and hence more seeds.

DEWBERRY.

LUCRETIA—This promises to be a great acquisition. The flowers are very large and showy. The fruit, which ripens with the Mammoth Cluster Raspberry, is often one and one-half inches long, by one inch in diameter, soft, sweet, and luscious throughout, without any hard center or core.

RASPBERRIES.

GOLDEN QUEEN—A deservedly praised novelty. Its large size, delicious flavor, beautiful appearance as a fruit, and its great vigor of growth and productiveness, place it in the front.

HILLBORN (Cap)—Originated in Canada and is undoubtedly the best black cap. It is full larger than Gregg and jet black in color. Is hardier and more productive.

TYLER—Best early cap.

OHIO—Good market cap.

TURNER—Very productive red, of good quality.

CUTHBERT—Probably the best red raspberry in cultivation.

STRAWBERRIES.

JESSIE--Heads the list as it is the leading berry for Wisconsin. It is our berry: was especially gotten up by Mr. London. of Janesville. Wisconsin. for our climate. It does not rust. It is a vigorous grower. Its many fruit stems are strong and carry the fruit well out of the dirt, but not above the luxuriant foliage. to allow it to sun-scald. It produces runners abundantly. The fruit is of ponderous size, and for so large a berry, very productive. Quality better than Crescent, no pithiness, but flesh solid and luscious throughout. It holds its size well to the 7th picking. Blossom perfect. Try it, every body.

BUBACH'S (No. 5)—Undoubtedly the next in value for our climate. Mr. Crawford says: "The plant is large, healthy, vigorous and very productive; leaves dark green and free from rust; runners strong and abundant; blossoms pistillate; (plant one row in five of Jessie); fruit very large and usually of good form." Originated in Princeton, Ill.

WARFIELD (No. 2)—We place this next in value of the new varieties. Originated in Illinois in 1883. Mr. Crawford, of Ohio, says: "It fruited in 1884, and a bed containing five square feet yielded a quart every other day. The blossom is pistillate. Plant vigorous with long penetrating roots to resist drouth. It ripens with the Crescent, has tall leaves to protect from late spring frosts. Single plants have produced 195 berries. It equals the Wilson as a shipper and is superior to it in every other respect. It has yielded one-half more than the Crescent with the same chance, and is far superior in every other way."

HAVERLAND —A seedling of the Crescent, originated in Ohio. Perfectly healthy plant, very vigorous, and wonderfully productive Berries very large, uniform in shape, and bright scarlet color. Quality not surpassed by any market berry. No rust; roots deep and fruit holds size well.

GANDY—The great late berry for Wisconsin. Is a good shipper and long keeper. Productive; never rusts or sun-scalds the fruit no matter how hot or wet the weather; of mammoth size, regular, bright scarlet, and perfect blossom.

We have the Crescent, May King, Jewell, Henderson, Cumberland, Belmont, Ontario, Gold, Monmouth, Logan, Bomba, Mammoth, Itasca, and twenty five others that will fruit this coming season. We are intending to compare and be able to advise as to the best to plant. I have fruited all but a few of the last mentioned varieties. Shall take great pains to furnish none but best plants, in fine condition. You will see by referring to the testimonials, that I understand packing.

DWARF JUNEBERRY.

This is becoming popular as a fruit for home growing, and I will have a limited supply of the plants the coming spring. I quote from Carpenter & Gage, of Nebraska: "For several years we have been watching the Juneberry, and

have come to the conclusion that it is one of
the most valuable berries, and it should be
planted on every farm in the west. The wood
is hard and firm and endures the extremes of
our climate without injury. Its leaves are dark,
glossy green, and very much resemble the pear.
The plant propagates from suckers. The flowers
appear about the same time as those of the
apple. The petals are white and five in number.
The fruit is borne in clusters like the currant,
and ripens in June. Its size equals the wild
gooseberry; shape, round; color, reddish purple at first and becomes a bluish black when
fully ripened. Its flavor approaches the huckle-
berry, a mild, very rich sub-acid. Most people
like its quality, and pronounce it delicious. It
may be served with sugar and cream or cooked
sauce, and is splendid canned for winter use.
The plant is about the height and form of the
currant bush. It produces fruit in enormous
quantities, and bears every year. It is also perfectly hardy, not being injured by wet, cold or
dry weather, and needs no special treatment.
Rabbits do not injure it, and it will grow readily
with only a scanty root."

ASPARAGUS.

To make a good Asparagus bed, the plants
may be set in the fall or early spring. Prepare
a place, by pulverizing the soil to a good depth
and dress liberally with fine manure Select
two-year, or strong one year plants, and for a
garden, set in rows 18 to 20 inches apart, with

plants 10 to 12 inches in the row. Make a hole by pressing the spade down perpendicularly and weaving it forward and back, draw it out and spread the roots with your fingers in fan shape and push down the spade two inches from where it went before and press towards the hole closing it. If in the fall, cover with several inches of coarse manure, and fork it in between the roots in the spring.

MOORE'S NEW CROSS-BRED—This new Asparagus is the result of careful cross-breeding between the Giant Improved and another excellent variety. It retains the head closed till the stalks are quite long; is of uniform color, while for tenderness and quality it is unparalleled. The size large, and remarkably uniform: a specimen bunch of twelve stalks weighed three pounds.

CONOVER'S COLOSSAL—Large, rapid growth, productive and of fine quality.

Ornamental Department.

EVERGREENS.

WE wish every farmer in the north-west could be made to see the benefit of a dense row of evergreens on the north and west sides of his farm and also a semi-circle extending from the south around westwardly to the north-east of his cattle and sheep yards, barns and all buildings. How few farms are thus protected. Let us look a moment at the benefits resulting from such wind-breaks outside of the idea of ornament. The belt of evergreens on the north and west boundaries of the farm will change the climate. You will find your Wisconsin or Minnesota farm has the climate of central Illinois, without the winds of the latter section. Your orchards will be improved often when that of the neighboring exposed farm will be badly demoralized. Why, do you say? March used to be considered the best month in which to season lumber because THE WINDS BLOW. Hard freezing tends to kiln dry wood, and frost will penetrate further if driven by a high wind, and evaporation is much more rapid. Hence an apple tree protected from the winds, will endure a much lower degree of temperature than if exposed. Your grain will not lodge so badly and your corn will not be blown down. The saving in this item some years would pay the first cost of the evergreen belt. The semi-circle about the yards and buildings saves at least one-fourth the feed of stock and at the same time is so much warmer and pleasanter for those who do the chores. Evergreens suitable for forming these belts, can be had for a small sum. They should be planted in a row, 6 feet apart in the row. 440 trees will plant 160 rods. For the lawn a few nice shaped evergreens are indispensable.

NORWAY SPRUCE—A lofty, elegant tree of perfect pyramidal habit. and the lower limbs retain their vigor with age. becoming gracefully pendulous as they grow old. The finest known evergreen as a single lawn tree and one of the best for protection belts and hedges.

WHITE SPRUCE—Our best native spruce. Is thought it will rival the popularity of the Norway. It is hardier and a lighter shade of green. Keeps its shape and lower branches as well as the Norway.

HEMLOCK SPRUCE—Is well known in its timber character where grown in dense masses, with no branches below 80 feet, but when grown in full sunlight as a single lawn tree, or in a group or ornamental hedges is truly unexcelled.

BALSAM FIR—A very regular, symmetrical tree, assuming the conical form when quite small. Spines dark, and silvery white underneath. It is fine in the lawn.   •

AMERICAN ARBOR VITAE—This is the best evergreen tree for ornamental hedges. Easily transplanted, flourishing under the closest shearing, and forms a very dense and beautiful hedge. Fine for cemetery adornment. Of course it was never adapted to turn stock; but forms a most desirable and ornamental screen to divide the lawn from other parts of the grounds, or make the boundary between residence lots in cities.

PARSON'S COMPACTA ARBOR VITAE—Foliage light green, habit dwarfish and quite compact. Hardy.

HOVEII ARBOR VITAE—A small globular shaped variety, naturally compact and very regular. Hardy.

PYRAMIDALIS ARBOR VITAE—The most beautiful of all the Arbor Vitæs, having dark green foliage, compact and erect form naturally. It fills the place of the Irish Juniper which is too tender here.

LITTLE GEM ARBOR VITAE—A very neat little dwarf, with fine foliage and compact, round head. Nice for the lawn—and cemetery.

WHITE PINE—This is without doubt one of the most valuable timber trees for the Northwest. It will do well on very light soils. It does not start as rapidly while young, but after ten years' planting is one of the fastest growers known. Fine for wind breakers.

MOUNTAIN PINE—A very dwarf species, compact. Foliage like the Scotch. Nice for lawn.

COLORADO BLUE SPRUCE—I quote from R. Douglas & Sons: "The Blue Spruce of Colorado, varies from dark green to light and dark blue in color. They are all beautiful, valuable and perfectly hardy, but the blue ones are the most admired. Specimen trees of the Blue Spruce, the Douglas Spruce of Colorado, and the White Spruce, from 20 to 30 feet high, in Massachusetts, Illinois, Iowa, Kansas and Nebraska, convince us that they will stand extreme drouth in summer and extreme cold in winter better than the common, so-called, hardy ever-greens."

We have a few Blue Spruce, 2½ feet, extra selected. Also the Douglas Spruce, 3 feet. They will fill EARLIEST orders.

Deciduous Trees.

WHITE ASH—Needs no description. Is one of the best trees for lawn or road line.

PURPLE-LEAVED BIRCH —With the habit of the Birches, it has beautiful purple foliage. Very desirable novelty.

CATALPA SPECIOSA--The hardy variety. A very ornamental and valuable tree. Seems to endure our worst winters.

AMERICAN LINDEN OR BASSWOOD—A rapid growing, beautiful native tree, with very large leaves and fragrant flowers. It is fine for lawn or road-side.

AMERICAN WHITE ELM –The noble drooping and spreading tree of our own woods. One of the grandest of Park or street trees.

NORWAY MAPLE—A foreign variety with large, broad leaves of a rich dark green. Probably the best maple in cultivation.

WIER'S CUT-LEAVED MAPLE—A Silver Maple with remarkable and beautifully dissected foliage. Of rapid growth, shoots slender and drooping, giving it a graceful appearance. Should be in every collection.

BOLIEANA POPLAR Lately introduced from Northern Russia. Does not sprout from the roots, is a very rapid grower, and is clean in habit. The leaves are almost black-green on the upper side and snow white underneath; when moved by the wind the trees present a most pleasing and unique appearance, distinct from all others. It is perfectly hardy.

CUT LEAVED WEEPING BIRCH—An elegant, erect tree, with slender, drooping branches and fine cut leaves. A magnificent variety and worthy a place on every lawn.

OREL WEEPING WILLOW—From Orel, Russia. New here, but destined to become very popular, from its persistently weeping habit and extreme hardiness.

WISCONSIN WEEPING WILLOW—Of drooping habit and perfectly hardy.

—

Deciduous Shrubs.

TARTARIAN HONEY-SUCKLE—Perfectly hardy, both red and white varieties. Flowers in May.

HYDRANGEA GRANDIFLORA—A fine large semi-shrub, with showy panicles of white flowers in the greatest profusion. Is very nearly hardy here, but is better to be borne down and covered with evergreen boughs or something to hold the snow. Valuable for massing on the lawn.

DEUTZIA SCABRA — Rough-leaved; profuse flowering, white.

DEUTZIA GRACILIS—A charming species from Japan. Flowers pure white, and very delicate in bloom and foliage.

SPIREAS —Are all elegant, low shrubs of easiest culture and perfectly hardy. Billardi is rose-colored; Prunifolia, little white daisy like flowers; Douglasii, spikes of deep rose-colored flowers in July; Ulmifolia, large round clusters of white flowers; Lanceolata, lance-pointed foliage, and large, round clusters of white flowers that cover the whole plant; a charming shrub; Reevesii, flowers white and double, blooms freely in clusters. One of the best of the Spireas

SYRINGA PHILADELPHUS — A well-known shrub, with white, fragrant flowers.

ROSES.

NOTHING gives better satisfaction than a bed of Roses in the lawn. In a circular bed eight feet in diameter, 75 plants would be required of the ever blooming, and 50 of the Hybrid Perpetuals and Mosses. The effect is very fine, composed of the different colors in mass. Handfuls of bloom may be gathered daily from June till frost, on the bed of ever-blooming varieties. It is almost impossible to feed a rose too highly, nor is there danger of pruning too much.

CLIMBING ROSES.

PRAIRIE QUEEN—Clear. bright pink, compact and globular, and very double.

BALTIMORE BELLE - Pale blush, very double and great bloomer.

PRIDE OF WASHINGTON-- Brilliant amaranth, shaded rose center. Large clusters, very double and fine.

MOSS ROSES.

CAPT. INGRAM—Brilliant carmine. large full flowers, mossy buds.

PRINCESS ADELAIDE—One of the best. Extra large flowers. color bright rosy pink, very double and fragrant. beautifully mossed.

LUXEMBOURG — Bright crimson. large and double, very sweet and mossy.

MADAM DUPUY - White. Splendid large flowers, very double, sweet and mossy.

EVER-BLOOMING ROSES.

AURORA—Full, medium size, very double and sweet. Color silvery rose. beautifully shaded with clear pink.

ALICE SISLEY—A splendid rose. Large, very full and double, exceedingly sweet. Color a rare shade of violet red. brightened with crimson maroon. Elegant large pointed buds.

BELLA—Pure snow white. large size, very full and double. Tea scented. Splendid pointed buds.

ISABELLA SPRUNT — Bright canary yellow. large beautiful buds, very sweet, tea scented. profuse bloomer.

PERLE DE LYON —Beautiful orange yellow with peach shading, sometimes coppery gold, stained with crimson. Charming buds and large, full flowers. Delicately perfumed.

HYBRID PERPETUAL ROSES.

BERNARD VARLET—A magnificent rose; large, full, globular form; color deep violet purple; free bloomer and very sweet.

ELIZA BOELDE —Very full and double, and delightfully perfumed. Color pure ivory white, sometimes clouded with blush and tinged with amber. Choice.

GEN. JACQUEMINOT — Rich velvety scarlet, changing to brilliant crimson. Magnificent buds.

PEONIE—One of the finest old roses. Never goes out of fashion Not excelled by any. Very large, full flowers. Clear bright red, very sweet.

MAD. LOUIS CARRIQUE —Rich velvety crimson. Large size, very double, full and sweet.

Have described a few representatives of the different colors, among the hundreds of fine sorts.

TESTIMONIALS.

From Hon. Samuel Wade, of Paonia, Colo., Seventy-five miles west of Leadville, May 3, 1888.

Dear Sir:—The 100 Jessie strawberry plants came to hand on the 1st inst., all right and I have them well set. The plants were good ones and in excellent condition.

From J. Max Clark, one of the most active members of the original Greeley colonists, Colorado, Sept. 29, 1888.

"Friend Tuttle:—I have neglected to reply to your notice of shipment of Jessie plants, until I should be able to set them out and see how they turned out. There happened to be no water in the ditch when they arrived, and as they seemed in good condition, I thought they would do better in the package until I could get water than they would do set in the dry earth with what sprinkling I could give them. You will observe that we wait for water in this country instead of rain and it being very low and scarce at this time of the year, we have to take turns and wait until we can get it. I set them out yesterday morning, and as I got the ground moistened around them I think they will do well. [They were shipped in open basket, Sept. 18, therefore ten days in the package. A. C. T.]

From Otto Wasserzieher, Deerwood, Minn., Sept. 1st, 1888.

"Dear Sir:—The Jessie strawberry plants received in excellent condition. I think it a wonderful idea to send plants raised in pots, with lumps of dirt, packed in moss, because every plant is sure to grow."

From Hon. J. B. Dwinnell, Lodi, Columbia Co., Wis., Sept. 20, 1888.

"Dear Sir:—The Jessie strawberry plants you sent me were received last Monday in fine order.

From H. H. Russell, Roslyn, Day Co., Dakota, Sept. 6, 1888.

Dear Sir:—The strawberry plants I got this morning and are planted. They were as fresh as if just taken out of their bed—could not be better.

From Mrs. J. S. Tripp, Prairie du Sac, Wis., Sept. 3, 1888.

"Dear Sir:—The strawberry plants arrived in prime condition. Not the least particle of earth was jarred from the roots. They were all, without exception, just as you removed them from the pots."

From N. F. Carpenter, Menominee, Wis., Aug. 27, 1888.

"Dear Sir:—The plants came through in No. 1 order."

From L. L. Inman, Havana, Steel County Minn., Aug. 30, 1888.

"Dear Sir:—The plants received all right. They were in nice shape. There are a number wanting plants, but I think they will now wait till next spring. Express charges $1.

From F. W. Wagner, Lansing, Iowa, May 2, 1888.

"Dear Sir:—The trees arrived all right and am well pleased with them."

From Milo Barnard, afterward Pres. Ills. State Hort. Soc., Manteno, Ills., Apr. 30, 1888.

"Dear Sir:—The apple trees came to hand to-day in excellent condition. Accept thanks for high grade, etc.

From J. B. Ellison, Taylor Station, Jackson Co., Wis., May 9, 1888.
Dear Sir: "The trees and berry bushes were duly received. I am very much obliged for the extras; they were just what I wanted.

From Dr. Elliott Brown, of Fond du Lac, Wis., Sept. 20, 1888.
Dear Sir:—The potted Jessie strawberry plants came in good time and fine condition. They look thrifty and healthy, and should all grow. The packing was well done and I could see no reason why they should not cross the continent in perfect order. Thanks. Most all the things are budding out and I think they all will.

From Geo. Wright, of Wrightsville, Wis., May 23, 1888.
"Dear Sir:—I received the trees and plants in splendid order and was well satisfied. You have done more than well by me. I set them all out in a favorable time and they seem to be doing well."

From C. F. McNair, Nurseryman, Dansville, N. Y., Aug. 29, 1887.
The apple buds were received in good condition, were budded promptly and have made a fine catch.

From Chas. Luedloff, Carver Co., Minn., Nov. 12, 1887.
"Dear Sir:—The trees you sent came to hand in excellent condition, never got better trees, and packing was done in the best manner. Many thanks. Your business shall have my recommendation to my neighbors."

From John Pool, Avon, Ills., Sept. 17, 1887.
"Dear Sir:—Your retail price list at hand. I have noticed it some. I will send you a list of what I want and if you can send me as good stock as I received from you last year and at the same price, I will order. This was a hard year; the drouth has been so hard on trees set last spring, everybody is discouraged. Your trees stood the best of any in this country." October 25, Mr. Pool says, "My bill of trees came to hand to day in good shape and I am well pleased with the stock."

From M. S. Fawcett, of Lyon Co., Minn.
"Dear Sir—I would say that the small bill of trees and shrubs I got from you last fall has done very well. All the blackberries grew and are nice. But a few of the raspberries grew, the Fay currants are very nice. I nursed the Moore's Early Grape vine all summer and it finally sprouted about the first of August and is now growing finely. When I want more trees, etc., I will send to you."

Norway Spruce.

Selected Stock at Low Rates.

The trees. plants, etc., described in this catalogue, I will furnish for this next spring's delivery (May,1889) at the following low prices. if ordered before March 1st 1889:

APPLES—Duchess and Wealthy, 4 to 6 feet.................15c.
   "   Whitney No. 20 Crab, 4 to 6 feet.................20c.
   "   New Russian except Vargul and Antonovka, 4 to 6 ft....25c.
   "   Vargul and Antonovka, 4 to 6 feet.................30c.
PLUMS—DeSoto. Wolf and Forest Garden. 4 to 6 feet.........50c.
CHERRIES—Wragg and Ostheim, 4 to 6 feet.................50c.
   "   Eng. Morello and E. Richmond, 4 to 6 feet ......35c.
GRAPES—Early Victor and Empire State ....50c.
   "   Brighton and Moore's Early..................30c.
   "   Worden..25c.
   "   Lady..40c.
   "   Concord.......................................10c.
CURRANTS—Fay's Prolific................................20c.
   "   Lee's Prolific..................................10c.
   "   White Grape.....................................5c.
   "   Victoria and LaVersailles ....5c.
   "   Long Bunch Holland..............................5c.
   "   Improved Red Dutch..............................4c.
GOOSEBERRIES—Downings ....15c.
   "   Smith's Improved................................15c.
JUNE BERRIES—Dwarf.....................................15c.
BLACKBERRIES—Snyder. Stone's Hardy and Ancient Briton..3c.
   "   Erie and Early King ....10c.
DEWBERRIES—Lucretia....................................5c.
RASPBERRIES—Hilborn B'k Cap............................5c.
   "   Ohio, Tyler, Souhegan and Gregg ....2c.
   "   Golden Queen...................................10c.
   "   Shaffers, Marlboro ....5c.
   "   Cuthbert and Turner.............................2c.
STRAWBERRIES—May King, Crescent... .....per dozen 25c.
   "   Wilson (true), Cumberland.......   "   25c.
   "   Bubach No. 5, and Haverland .   "   50c.
   "   Jessie and Warfield No. 2.......   "   75c.
EVERGREENS—Norway Spruce and Balsam Fir, 2 to 3 feet ...30c.
   "   American Arbor Vitæ, 3 feet....................30c.
   "   Hemlock, extra stocky, 2 feet ....35c.
   "   Pyramidalis.Arbor Vitæ ....$1.00.
   "   Little Gem ....75c.
   "   Siberian   "   " ....50c.
   "   Mountain Pine..................................50c.
ROSES—Climbing ....25c.
   "   Moss...35c.
   "   Hybrid Perpetual...............................35c.

1889

DESCRIPTIVE CATALOGUE

OF

ADAPTED FRUIT TREES

SMALL FRUITS, PLANTS, ETC.

A. G. TUTTLE,

BARABOO, WI—

SPRING AND FALL

➤*DIRECTIONS. ✛ TERMS. ✛ ETC.*◄

———➤❧ O ❧◄———

PLEASE order early, before any varieties are exhausted and you will then get what you want. If you leave the selection of varieties to me I will use my best judgment in the choice. Tell me what your soil is; the location as to elegation, slope, protection, etc. Also state your troubles in growing fruit and I will aid you all I can

Please write your name plainly, giving the post office, express office, county and state. Also the name of the railway. Enclose the amount of the bill, and I will do my best to suit you. If any claim is made it should be sent inside ten days to receive attention. We deliver all packages to the forwarders free, and then our control ceases and of course our responsibility also. Look to the forwarders for all damages occurring en route. Packing is done in the best possible manner. We make it a point to pack as light as possible and at the same time insure the best condition of the stock. All goods are packed free and everything tied and labeled distinctly.

Mistakes sometimes occur. We warrant our stock to be true to name with the express understanding that if any proves untrue, we will replace it with other, but in no case will we be liable for damages

This is a stationary institution and can be found. Its guarantee is worth something. Its reputation for furnishing "pedigree" stock adapted to the North-west cost toil and expense and is to be maintained. When we sell short we do not order Alabama stock to fill orders. Try us.

Remit by postoffice money order on Baraboo, express money order, registered letter or draft, but no postage stamps, postal notes or private checks. Address all letters to

A. G. TUTTLE,
Baraboo, Wis.

INTRODUCTORY.

N this day of the world it is said to be nearly impossible to sell anything except by personal solicitation. The wholesale grocer of the larger cities has commercial solicitors traveling from one customer to another. The tree-grower must send out his agents to solicit the trade, or his competitor will get it. It has become almost impossible to get any mail orders. Do the people get any better goods? Do they find the prices better? Is the peddler any more reliable than the nurseryman? Is there any advantage gained by giving the orders to the first smooth tongued traveler, instead of mailing it to the nearest nurseryman noted for honest deal and honest goods? I employ no agents or traveling men, but am obliged to wholesale to those who sell direct to the planter. I would much prefer to receive the orders from the planter, and he would be the gainer EVERY TIME. I know of parties within two miles of this nursery, who have bought bills of trees several times of irresponsible traveling treemen, and they probably will again. They pay three times the prices that live trees of the same varieties would cost at this nursery, and they have the vacant orchard rows to show for the ducats expended. They are the people who are so loud in de-nouncing Wisconsin as totally incapable of producing fruit, now and forever. This catalogue is not for that class of persons. It is for those who would like to raise fruit, and buy intending to do their part towards making their purchases a success; who take a live, progressive, instructive, high-toned horticultural journal like the "Popular Gardening" of Buffalo. N. Y.. and read it and profit by its reliable teachings. We hope to prove to these parties that OUR STOCK IS RELIABLE. That our advice as to what is best to plant is valuable. That our way of doing business is not only pleasant but profitable to our customers. To our old customers we are grateful, and to the new ones, we will promise the strictest attention to their wants, hoping to add all their names to our long list of kind friends who buy of us because they have found it paid them to do so. TRY US with a small order.

On receipt of your trees if they appear to be dry, bury them TOPS AND ALL, in moist earth for a few days. If it has been freezing weather and you have reason to think there is frost in them, put the package, UNOPENED, into a dark cellar, for a day or two, and let the frost come out gradually, and if the roots were well mossed in packing. they will be uninjured. When Strawberries are received and you are not quite ready to plant them, be sure that the roots are kept moist. without moistening the foliage, and put them on the cellar bottom. Evergreens *must be kept from drying the roots in the least.* Heel them in as fast as unpacked and not allow the sun or wind to reach the bare roots for a moment. A good way is to prepare a clay puddle and immerse the roots, which will give them a coating that will exclude sun and air. Then heel them in. After the sap of an evergreen once hardens it never flows again. The tree is dead, though the foliage may not show it for many days.

BURYING TREES.

SELECT a spot where the water does not stand. Dig an open trench long enough to take the trees laid singly, side by side, with roots in the trench and tops along the ground, at right angles with the trench. Cut Roman numerals in the back of the labels, and mark the same against the name in your book record, as the moist earth will take out the pencil marks. Then open each variety and place them, driving a stake between each variety. After all are in, throw fine earth, free from all rubbish, among and on the roots, shaking and tramping enough to fill all interstices among the roots. Cover roots one foot and slant off to the tops, covering the extreme tops about three inches. Put no straw or other rubbish on or near them to attract mice. In the Spring open carefully with a fork, not to gall the trunks or break the branches, and plant *as soon as the frost is out sufficiently.*

COLLECTIONS.

-

THE following collections will be selected from the best stock, and will be nicely packed in moss and burlaps, each variety being tied separately and labeled. We make no changes in the contents of any package. Please order by the numbers. Any three $1.00 collections for $2.50. Any two $3 00 collections for $5.00:

No. 1. 1 Transparent Apple, 4 to 6 feet 30
        1 Switzer   "   "   30
        1 Zolotoref   "   "   30
        1 Longfield   "   "   30

                                                          $1.20

No. 2. 1 Anis   "   "   30
        1 Hibernal   "   "   30
        1 Lord's   "   "   30
        1 Repka Malenka Apple   "   30

                                                          $1.20

No. 3. 1 Blackwood Apple   "   35
        1 Vargul   "   "   40
        1 Antonovka   "   "   50

                                                          $1.25

No. 4. 1 Whitney No. 20 Crab   "   25
        1 Ostheim Cherry   "   50
        1 DeSoto Plum   "   50

                                                          $1.25

No. 5. 1 Early Victor Grape 50
        1 Moore's Early Grape 50
        1 Concord Grape   25

                                                          $1.25

No. 6. 1 Moore's Early Grape 50
        1 Worden Grape   30
        1 Brighton Grape   40

                                                          $1.20

No. 7. 1 Early Victor Grape. 50
        1 Empire State Grape 75

                                                          $1.25

No. 8.   2 Fay Currant 50
         2 White Grape Currant 12
         2 Victoria Currant 12
         2 Cherry Currant 12
         2 La Versailes Currant 12
         2 Lee's Prolific Currant 25
                                            ——
                                            $1.23

No. 9.   3 Downing Gooseberry.... 60
         3 Smith's Improved Gooseberry.......... 70
                                                 ——
                                                 $1.30

No 10.   5 Lucretia Dewberry 40
         10 Ancient Briton Blackberry 30
         10 Stone's Hardy " 30
         10 Snyder   " 30
                                            ——
                                            $1 30

No. 11. 5 Hilborn (Black Cap) Raspberry 30
         10 Tyler (Black Cap) Raspberry 25
         10 Ohio (Black Cap) Raspberry... 25
         10 Turner Raspberry 25
         10 Cuthbert Raspberry................... 25
                                                 ——
                                                 $1.30

No. 12. 10 Jessie Strawberry...... , ... 40
         10 Bubach No. 5, Strawberry............. 30
         10 Warfield No. 2, Strawberry.......... 40
         10 Wilson (Pure)....................... 20
                                                 ——
                                                 $1.30

Any of the foregoing numbers for $1.00. Any of the following numbers for $3.00:

No. 1.   12 New Russian Apple Trees, 4 to 6 feet, of our
         selection of 4 sorts $3.60

No. 2.   6 New Russian Apple 4 to 6 feet........... 1.80
         2 English Morello Cherry 60
         1 Wragg Cherry 60
         2 Whitney No 20, Crab 50
                                                     ——
                                                     $3.50

No. 3.   2 Vargul Apples 4 to 6 feet..... 80
         2 Antonovka 4 to 6 feet 1.00
         2 DeSoto Plum, 4 to 6 feet 1.00
         1 Forest Garden Plum, 4 to 6 feet ... .,. ... 50
         1 English Morello Cherry 30
                                                      ——
                                                      $3.60

No. 4.   2 Moore's Early Grape 1.00
         2 Worden   "   60
         2 Brighton   "   80
         2 Lady   " 1.00
         1 Concord   "   25

                                                          $3.65
No. 5.   5 Fay Currant....   ....   1.25
         5 White Grape Currant   30
         6 Lucretia Dewberry   48
         ient Briton Blackberry................   30
         10 Stone's Hardy   "   30
         10 Tyler Raspberry   25
         2 Downing Gooseberry...   48
         2 Smith's Improved Gooseberry....   40

                                                          $3.68
No. 6.   50 Jessie Strawberry 1.50
         50 Haverland Strawberry........... ......   1.50
         25 Bubach No. 5 Strawberry.   60

                                                          $3.60
No. 7.   8 Norway Spruce 2½ feet, for $3.00
No. 8.   8 Balsam Fir, 3 feet, for $3.00
No. 9.   8 White Spruce, 2 feet, for 3.00
No. 10. 2 Norway Spruce, 2½ feet 1.00
         2 Balsam Fir, 3 feet 1.00
         2 White Spruce, 2 feet   75
         2 American Arbor Vitæ, 2 feet   75

                                                          $3.50
No. 12. 1 Pyramidalis Arbor Vitæ 1.00
         1 Little Gem   "   " 1.00
         1 Mountain Pine   50
         1 Cut-leaved Weeping Birch 1.00

                                                          $3.50

APPLES.

TWENTY-TWO years ago we obtained our first scions from Russia, and for more than fifteen years have had the new Russians in orchard. We planted at the same time an orchard of 300 Duchess. The per cent. of in this orchard is ten times greater than in an orchard of 80 varieties of new Russians growing near it. The only trees killed by the winter of 1884-5, of the new Russians. are two Crimean apples and one that came to us as Green Transparent, which proved to be White Astrachan. Some eight or ten varieties have proved worthless by blight. Of the 300 Duchess 20 were killed outright by that winter, and many others more or less injured. In sending to Russia for scions, we hoped to get at least a dozen varieties as hardy as the Duchess, and fruit that would successfully compete in the markets with the old favorites of the East. The results of the tests we have made, abundantly prove that very many of the new Russians are hardier than the Duchess and equal in quality to any of the old American sorts, giving us fruit in season from *very early to very late.* The only thing in the way of the general planting of the new Russian fruits, is the loss of confidence in them occasioned by the dissemination by some Wisconsin and Minnesota nurserymen, of trees purporting to be Russians, which *were grown in Alabama.*

Before discarding the Russians we would ask the planters of Wisconsin to make a trial of, at least, a few of our trees. If you will leave the selection to us, we think we can furnish you trees that will succeed. Our stock is grown here. The scions are taken from the trees which have borne, and consequently *must be true to name.* Try a dozen.

TRANSPARENT—Mr. Lovett, of New Jersey, says: "It ripens fully ten days in advance of the Early Harvest, and the past season I picked fully ripe specimens on the 30th of June. Size medium; light transparent lemon yellow, smooth waxen surface: flesh melting, juicy and of excellent quality, and for an early apple, an exceptionally good keeper and shipper—surpassing far in these important points Early Harvest, Primate and other early varieties. Tree a free upright grower, very prolific and a remarkably early bearer, frequently producing in the nursery row, the second year from the bud.

YELLOW SWEET—Earlier than Transparent. Tree a fine grower and very hardy. Fruit yellow with reddish bronze on the sun side; flesh firm and agreeably sweet, good for dessert and cooking. Keeps well for so early an apple.

EARLY GLASS—Tree is extremely hardy and free from blight—never loses a bud from severity of climate—is a fine and regular grower and good bearer. Fruit self colored, with little color on sun side. Good bearer and keeps well if picked before over-ripe.

ENORMOUS—The largest of August apples. Some specimens have been grown here measuring 14 inches in circumference. Almost covered with deep red, it is very showy. Flesh a little coarse but a good sub-acid flavor. Season, August and September.

PROLIFIC SWEETING—A yellow apple of medium to large size. Dr. Hoskins says the "best of the sweet apples for market purposes." Tree, a very stocky grower and great bearer. Is hardy at St. Petersburg.

CHARLAMOFF—A very large yellow apple, mildly acid, ripens at the end of August. A good grower and productive. Season, September.

SWITZER—Tree very hardy, handsome, upright grower, and very productive. Fruit medium to large, entirely covered with red. Flesh white, fine-grained, tender, sub-acid, with a delightful quince-like flavor. An excellent keeper for its season, and one of the best fall apples. October.

VASILIS LARGEST—This belongs to the same family as Green Streaked, and Zolotoref, a little more color perhaps and tree a little more upright. October and November.

ARABIAN—As received from the department is of the Duchess type of apple, but a little better keeper. A remarkably free grower in the nursery, and makes a very symmetrical orchard tree. October.

BEAUTIFUL ARCADE--Tree an upright, pretty grower in the nursery, in the orchard more spreading. Very hardy. Fruit above medium size, delicately striped with pink on light green. Flesh white, tender, juicy, very pleasant sweet. Dessert and cooking. November.

GREEN STREAKED—A very large showy apple, striped with red, somewhat coarse in texture, but a salable apple, that keeps into winter. Distinct green veinings in the flesh are characteristic and probably suggested the name. Season, October to January.

GLASS GREEN—As received by me from the Department, is an improved Duchess. Is hardier and much better nursery grower, and the fruit is a milder acid and keeps till November.

RASPBERRY—A beautiful little bright red, dessert apple. A very pleasant, fresh and sprightly sub-acid, with a nice after taste. Flesh white with scarlet veins near the skin. Tree, upright and vigorous, and stands the worst winters at St. Petersburg without injury. Its beauty and fine flavor, and the perfect hardiness of the tree, will command favor wherever planted. October to January.

HEIDORNS STREAKED—A very beautiful large sized apple, dull red splashed on yellow, very sweet and of delicate texture. Dr. Regel, of St. Petersburg, says: It bears a large amount of fruit every year, and stands the climate of St. Petersburg. Please note that St. Petersburg is in 60 degrees north latitude, or 1,136 miles north of this place. Season, October to January.

YELLOW ARCADE—A yellow apple with a little red on the sun side. Flesh tender, juicy, slight sub-acid. Dessert and cooking. November.

GOLDEN WHITE—Fruit is medium to large, with no cavity. In color a dull green turning to yellow with some show of red striping on the sun side; basin bronzed and russeted. Flesh tender; flavor a mild acid. Tree rather slow in the nursery, but vigorous in the orchard, and a great and annual bearer. Buds very wooly and prominent. Season, November and December.

BARLOFF—Of the Alexander type as to size, shape and color. Flesh white and agreeably vinous-sweet. Is a nice grower and productive. Will undoubtedly become popular as an early winter sweet apple. Season, November and December.

ZOLOTOREFF—Undoubtedly the best of the large fall apples. A large, cylindrical, showy apple; deep red, with splashes of dark green in the basin. Flesh a little coarse, but juicy and spicy, with an agreeable after taste. Season, November to January.

LITTLE HAT—Dr. Regel says: "A globular fruit of full medium size. On the sunny side a pale blush with a good deal of dark red in stripes and splashes. Flesh greenish-white, juicy and a little sweet. A good looking fruit which ripens in September, and keeps through December. For house use only." Tree is a remarkably fine grower in the nursery, and perfectly hardy. November.

JUICY BURR—A very hardy tree and nice grower. Fruit resembles the Duchess in size, shape and color, but better quality and keeps through November.

WATERMELON—A very strong grower. Stands perfectly the climate of St. Petersburg. Fruit one of the largest, somewhat oblong in shape. Color yellow with light and dark crimson stripes.

Flesh greenish white, with an agreeable acid taste. A fine looking dessert and cooking apple. November.

RED ANIS—When Mr. Gibb questioned the people of Russia, as to which was the hardiest apple, they invariably replied: "Anis." Fruit a medium sized, flat apple. Color, dark carmine with some dingy yellow on the shady side. Flesh greenish white, juicy and sour. Keeps until January.

LONG ARCADE—A medium sized apple, much like Red Astrachan in form and color. Flesh, white and fine grained; flavor, a mild pleasant acid. Tree good grower and very hardy, bearing quite young. Season. December and January.

CZAR'S THORN—A sweet apple, oblong, of large size. Color, red on yellow. Tree is very hardy and a profuse bearer. December to January.

WHITE APPLE—Size medium. Greenish yellow, all one color. Flesh white, sub-acid, tender and juicy, with an agreeable, vinous acid flavor. Good for kitchen and dessert. Tree endures, uninjured, the worst winters of St. Petersburg. December to January.

SKROUT GERMAN—A very pretty, regular grower in the nursery and forms a beautiful orchard tree. Very productive and does not blight much. Fruit above medium, regular in shape, pale yellow with considerable red on the sun-side, and light and dark carmine stripes. Flesh is fine grained, tender and juicy, an agreeable, vinous acid. One of the best for dessert and kitchen. January.

ZUSOFF—Tree a fine, upright grower in the nursery and more spreading in the orchard. Very productive. Fruit medium, bright red, hangs well on the tree. Flesh crisp, juicy pleasant sub-acid. Fine for dessert, showy on the table. Good shipper. January.

KOURSK'S ANIS—One of the best of the Anis family. Tree a good grower and very hardy. Fruit above medium in size and keeps through January. Flesh yellowish white, pleasant acid. Good dessert apple.

LONGFIELD—An early winter apple of fine quality and very attractive in appearance, having a bright carmine cheek, gradually fading into the most beautiful peach blush, and then into a delicate waxen lemon color. A fine basket fruit. Dr. Regel says: "Neither the cold, nor the winds, nor the storms of the intensely Steppe climate of Serepta, have disturbed the growth of this tree. Of 100 different varieties growing in the garden of Mr. Langerfield—from whom the name—only this one bears fruit every year." It is a prodigious and very regular bearer, is a somewhat irregular grower in the nursery, but soon becomes a shapely tree in the orchard. Season January.

WHITE PIGEON—An extra hardy tree and good bearer. Fruit medium size, conic in form with wrinkled eye and no basin. Sweet, with peculiar but pleasant flavor, tender and juicy. January and February.

HIBERNAL—A valuable early winter variety, large and showy, light yellow, striped and blotched with red. Quite acid and very good for cooking. Tree hardy and superb grower. Season January and February.

BLACKWOOD—A favorite winter dessert apple on the Volga and commands an extra price on account of its fine quality. Medium size, greenish yellow with a little red. Flesh white, tender, juicy, agreeably vinous acid, with a very pleasant aftertaste. A good dessert and kitchen apple which keeps through February.

BORSDORFER—Is an apple of German origin about as hardy as the Wealthy, but of such fine quality as to warrant a trial in favorable locations. Ask a German about the Borsdorfer and he will tell you "It is the best apple that ever was." Fruit below medium in size, form and color resembles Ben Davis, flesh firm and of fine texture, sub-acid, rich and very good. Keeps through the winter.

RED QUEEN—Good grower and very hardy. Fruit medium to large, dark green with dull red on the sunside. Good shipping. March.

VARGUL—One of the most popular apples in Russia. When mature is a light yellow, with a reddish brown on the sunside, covering one-third the apple. Is large, to quite large and ribbed. Flesh yellowish white, soft, juicy, rich sub-acid and very nice after taste. Its fine size and excellent flavor recommends it among the best. Is extremely hardy and as yet no blight. March.

LORD'S APPLE—This is one of the best of the new Russians we have tested. Tree hardy and fine grower. Fruit large; shape, size, color and bloom resembles the Blue Pearmain and keeps as well. A clear, strong but pleasant acid, hangs well on the tree and bears abundantly. Stands the most trying winters of St. Petersburg. March and April.

REPKA MALENKA—One of the valuable new Russian apples from its keeping qualities, as it has kept till the June of the second year, with ordinary care. Mr. Webster, of Vermont, says, "It is an enormous biennial bearer. It is too hard to eat until warm weather in the spring, when it gradually ripens and becomes tender, spicy and of good quality and flavor." Mr. Sias says of it at winter meeting of Minnesota Horticultural Society, in Feb., 1886: "It was the best keeper shown. It tasted fresh and tart as if fresh picked from the tree." March and onward.

ANTONOVKA—This is the "King apple of the Russian steppes." Dr. Regel says, "This is one of the most highly prized and widely grown apples in Russia. It grows in the northern part of the Province of St. Petersburg, at Valaam, along the Baltic Sea and in eastern Russia. It is sub-acid, with an agreeable after taste; firm and juicy. It keeps till July, and is a delicate dessert fruit. This tree grows so readily in the far North, and has such a combination of good points, that many grow scarcely anything else. It is very much liked by the people, and brings the highest prices."

Beside the foregoing new Russian apples, we have the

WEALTHY—Minnesota's well known seedling. Fruit medium to large, oblate, skin very smooth, whitish yellow, shaded with deep red in the sun, and spotted in the shade. Flesh white, firm, tender, juicy, lively sub-acid; very good. December to February.

DUCHESS OF OLDENBURG —So well known as to need no description. It is still the fruit from which points of hardiness are graded in the north-west.

ORANGE WINTER—An apple which originated in this county. The original tree has now stood in quite sandy soil since 1850 and is perfectly healthy, bearing regular crops of fruit alternate years. Fruit is above medium in size, a light green and yellow, with red on one side. Flesh is yellowish white, rich, fine-grained, pleasant sub-acid and keeps through the winter.

WHITNEY (No. 20) **CRAB**—The best of all the crab apples, but should be gathered as soon as the seeds are black. The finest grower in the nursery, and makes a very symmetrical orchard tree. Great and regular bearer. Fruit three times the size of Transcendent; carmine with darker stripes. Nice fruit to eat from the tree.

CHERRIES.

OSTHEIM—A new variety which is very generally raised in Russia and endures the climate of Vladimir. It is above medium in size, sweet and rich, a good bearer and perfectly healthy. 4 to 6 feet, well branched.

WRAGG—Is a valuable seedling originated in Iowa. It is proving to be valuable for the north-west, as it is hardy and healthy; bears well. Fruit good size and pleasant as a dessert fruit.

English Morello, Early Richmond and Late Kentish are old sorts well known.

PLUMS

DE SOTO—Originated in Wisconsin, of native blood. Is very hardy, healthy and productive. Fruit nearly as large as the Lombard, freestone, solid fleshed, rich and sweet.

FOREST GARDEN—Ripens a little in advance of the De Soto, which it closely resembles in tree and is as hardy and healthy. Fruit something like the Yellow Egg in appearance.

WOLF—Originated in Iowa and is one of the best for the north-west. It is a dark red, solid fleshed fruit, and great bearer.

Also the **MINER**, which is proving valuable where of sufficient age, as it does not bear young.

GRAPES.

EARLY VICTOR—Season of the Janesville but much better fruit. Black. Bunch and berry medium, cluster compact. Tender, sweet, rich and very good.

MOORE'S EARLY—Two weeks earlier than the Concord. Should be in every collection.

BRIGHTON—Dark red. One of the most desirable of the new grapes. Ripens with the Worden.

EMPIRE STATE—A very strong grower. Best of the white grapes. Earlier than Concord. Keeps well.

LADY—A very choice white grape. Healthy but not as vigorous as the Empire State. Fruit nice size and very fine quality.

WORDEN—Black. Bunch and berry large. Quality much better than Concord and a week earlier. For home use it is one of the very best of the blacks.

CURRANTS.

Currants require the best of cultivation and high feed. The fence corner theory of old times, is—we are glad to say—discarded. The worms have weeded out the shiftless and careless growers, and the enterprising ones soon found it paid to feed and cultivate this wholesome fruit.

Plant your currants in rows six feet apart, and three feet in the row, keep clean from weeds, and top dress occasionally with rotten manure, and when the worms appear, dust the foliage thoroughly with powdered White Hellebore while the dew is on, repeating it after three days. This if attended to promptly, will exterminate the last worm.

FAY'S PROLIFIC—This is truly a great advance in currants. It is all the most enthusiastic claim for it. Equals the cherry in size of berry, in bunch twice the size, better in flavor, with much less acid, and five times as productive and from its peculiar stem, is less expensive to pick. The cherry currant has been sold very generally for the Fay's, and it has damaged its character. I get my stock direct from the introducer at Fredonia, N. Y., and *know it is true*.

WHITE GRAPE — The best white currant. Bunches large and long, berry large and of the best quality, being less acid than others. Prolific and strong grower.

VICTORIA—A valuable variety, ripening as it does after all others are gone. Bunches very long, berry of medium size, brilliant red and of excellent quality. Bushes good growers and profuse bearers. No collection should be without it.

IMPROVED RED DUTCH—Is a great improvement over the well known Red Dutch, in size of berry and bunch.

LEE'S PROLIFIC—A black variety of recent introduction and one that marks a great advance in the Blacks. It is earlier than the Naples, with very large berries, longer and larger clusters, and even more prolific than that productive variety.

BERRIES.

GOOSEBERRIES.

DOWNING—Fruit larger than Houghton; nice, upright, stocky grower, almost entirely free from mildew. Roundish, light green, with distinct veins: skin smooth, flesh rather soft, juicy and very good.

SMITH'S IMPROVED—From Vermont. Large, oval, light green, with bloom: flesh moderately firm, sweet and good. Vigorous grower.

BLACKBERRIES.

One of the most profitable fruits to grow for market. Plant in rows eight feet apart and three feet in the row. Give the best of cultivation and high feed. Pinch back all new canes when they reach 18 inches and the arms at 12 inches. Keep the crop as near the ground as possible. Treat all sprouts as weeds. Cover in the winter, after bearing down the canes carefully and putting on a spade or two of earth to hold them down, with evergreen boughs or corn stalks.

SNYDER—Is too well known to need a description, but is the earliest of the trio, viz: Snyder. Ancient Briton and Stone's Hardy.

ANCIENT BRITON—Is probably the most profitable blackberry grown. In quality, is first-class. Productiveness not excelled if equalled. Should plant three-fourths of this variety, one-eighth Snyder for early and one-eighth Stone's Hardy for late.

STONE'S HARDY—Keeps up well the character of its predecessor in the season. The drupes are not quite as large as those in the Ancient Briton and hence more seeds.

DEWBERRY.

LUCRETIA—This promises to be a great acquisition. The flowers are very large and showy. The fruit, which ripens with the Mammoth Cluster Raspberry, is often one and one-half inches long, by one inch in diameter, soft, sweet, and luscious throughout, without any hard center or core.

RASPBERRIES.

GOLDEN QUEEN—A deservedly praised novelty. Its large size, delicious flavor, beautiful appearance as a fruit, and its great vigor of growth and productiveness, place it in the front.

HILLBORN (Cap)—Originated in Canada and is undoubtedly the best black cap. It is full larger than Gregg and jet black in color. Is hardier and more productive.

TYLER—Best early cap.

OHIO—Good market cap.

TURNER—Very productive red, of good quality.

CUTHBERT—Probably the best red raspberry in cultivation.

STRAWBERRIES.

JESSIE--Heads the list as it is the leading berry for Wisconsin. It is our berry; was especially gotten up by Mr. London, of Janesville, Wisconsin, for our climate. It does not rust. It is a vigorous grower. Its many fruit stems are strong and carry the fruit well out of the dirt, but not above the luxuriant foliage, to allow it to sun-scald. It produces runners abundantly. The fruit is of ponderous size, and for so large a berry, very productive. Quality better than Crescent, no pithiness, but flesh solid and luscious throughout. It holds its size well to the 7th picking. Blossom perfect. Try it, every body.

BUBACH'S (No. 5)--Undoubtedly the next in value for our climate. Mr. Crawford says: "The plant is large, healthy, vigorous and very productive; leaves dark green and free from rust; runners strong and abundant; blossoms pistillate; (plant one row in five of Jessie); fruit very large and usually of good form." Originated in Princeton. Ill.

WARFIELD (No. 2)--We place this next in value of the new varieties. Originated in Illinois in 1883. Mr. Crawford, of Ohio, says: "It fruited in 1884, and a bed containing five square feet yielded a quart every other day. The blossom is pistillate. Plant vigorous with long penetrating roots to resist drouth. It ripens with the Crescent, has tall leaves to protect from late spring frosts. Single plants have produced 195 berries. It equals the Wilson as a shipper and is superior to it in every other respect. It has yielded one-half more than the Crescent with the same chance, and is far superior in every other way."

HAVERLAND—A seedling of the Crescent, originated in Ohio. Perfectly healthy plant, very vigorous, and wonderfully productive Berries very large, uniform in shape, and bright scarlet color. Quality not surpassed by any market berry. No rust: roots deep and fruit holds size well.

GANDY—The great late berry for Wisconsin. Is a good shipper and long keeper. Productive: never rusts or sun-scalds the fruit no matter how hot or wet the weather: of mammoth size, regular, bright scarlet, and perfect blossom.

We have the Crescent, May King, Jewell, Henderson, Cumberland, Belmont, Ontario, Gold, Monmouth, Logan, Bomba, Mammoth, Itasca, and twenty-five others that will fruit this coming season. We are intending to compare and be able to advise as to the best to plant. I have fruited all but a few of the last mentioned varieties. Shall take great pains to furnish none but best plants, in fine condition. You will see by referring to the testimonials, that I understand packing.

DWARF JUNEBERRY.

This is becoming popular as a fruit for home growing, and I will have a limited supply of the plants the coming spring. I quote from Carpenter & Gage, of Nebraska: "For several years we have been watching the Juneberry, and

have come to the conclusion that it is one of
the most valuable berries, and it should be
planted on every farm in the west. The wood
is hard and firm and endures the extremes of
our climate without injury. Its leaves are dark,
glossy green, and very much resemble the pear.
The plant propagates from suckers. The flowers
appear about the same time as those of the
apple. The petals are white and five in number.
The fruit is borne in clusters like the currant,
and ripens in June. Its size equals the wild
gooseberry; shape, round; color, reddish purple at first and becomes a bluish black when
fully ripened. Its flavor approaches the huckle-
berry, a mild, very rich sub-acid. Most people
like its quality, and pronounce it delicious. It
may be served with sugar and cream or cooked
sauce, and is splendid canned for winter use.
The plant is about the height and form of the
currant bush. It produces fruit in enormous
quantities, and bears every year. It is also perfectly hardy, not being injured by wet, cold or
dry weather, and needs no special treatment.
Rabbits do not injure it, and it will grow readily
with only a scanty root."

ASPARAGUS.

To make a good Asparagus bed, the plants
may be set in the fall or early spring. Prepare
a place, by pulverizing the soil to a good depth
and dress liberally with fine manure Select
two-year, or strong one year plants, and for a
garden, set in rows 18 to 20 inches apart, with

plants 10 to 12 inches in the row. Make a hole by pressing the spade down perpendicularly and weaving it forward and back, draw it out and spread the roots with your fingers in fan shape and push down the spade two inches from where it went before and press towards the hole closing it. If in the fall, cover with several inches of coarse manure, and fork it in between the roots in the spring.

MOORE'S NEW CROSS-BRED—This new Asparagus is the result of careful cross-breeding between the Giant Improved and another excellent variety. It retains the head closed till the stalks are quite long; is of uniform color, while for tenderness and quality it is unparalleled. The size large, and remarkably uniform; a specimen bunch of twelve stalks weighed three pounds.

CONOVER'S COLOSSAL—Large, rapid growth, productive and of fine quality.

Ornamental Department.

EVERGREENS.

WE wish every farmer in the north-west could be made to see the benefit of a dense row of evergreens on the north and west sides of his farm and also a semi-circle extending from the south around westwardly to the north-east of his cattle and sheep yards, barns and all buildings. How few farms are thus protected. Let us look a moment at the benefits resulting from such wind-breaks outside of the idea of ornament. The belt of evergreens on the north and west boundaries of the farm will change the climate. You will find your Wisconsin or Minnesota farm has the climate of central Illinois, without the winds of the latter section. Your orchards will be improved often when that of the neighboring exposed farm will be badly demoralized. Why, do you say? March used to be considered the best month in which to season lumber because THE WINDS BLOW. Hard freezing tends to kiln-dry wood, and frost will penetrate further if driven by a high wind, and evaporation is much more rapid. Hence an apple tree protected from the winds, will endure a much lower degree of temperature than if exposed. Your grain will not lodge so badly and your corn will not be blown down. The saving in this item some years would pay the first cost of the evergreen belt. The semi-circle about the yards and buildings, saves at least one-fourth the feed of stock and at the same time is so much warmer and pleasanter for those who do the chores. Evergreens suitable for forming these belts, can be had for a small sum. They should be planted in a row, 6 feet apart in the row. 440 trees will plant 160 rods. For the lawn a few nice shaped evergreens are indispensable.

NORWAY SPRUCE—A lofty, elegant tree of perfect pyramidal habit, and the lower limbs retain their vigor with age, becoming gracefully pendulous as they grow old. The finest known evergreen as a single lawn tree and one of the best for protection belts and hedges.

WHITE SPRUCE—Our best native spruce. Is thought it will rival the popularity of the Norway. It is hardier and a lighter shade of green. Keeps its shape and lower branches as well as the Norway.

HEMLOCK SPRUCE—Is well known in its timber character where grown in dense masses, with no branches below 80 feet, but when grown in full sunlight as a single lawn tree, or in a group or ornamental hedges is truly unexcelled.

BALSAM FIR—A very regular, symmetrical tree, assuming the conical form when quite small. Spines dark, and silvery white underneath. It is fine in the lawn.

AMERICAN ARBOR VITAE—This is the best evergreen tree for ornamental hedges. Easily transplanted, flourishing under the closest shearing, and forms a very dense and beautiful hedge. Fine for cemetery adornment. Of course it was never adapted to turn stock; but forms a most desirable and ornamental screen to divide the lawn from other parts of the grounds, or make the boundary between residence lots in cities.

PARSON'S COMPACTA ARBOR VITAE—Foliage light green. habit dwarfish and quite compact. Hardy.

HOVEII ARBOR VITAE—A small globular shaped variety, naturally compact and very regular. Hardy.

PYRAMIOALIS ARBOR VITAE—The most beautiful of all the Arbor Vitæs, having dark green foliage, compact and erect form naturally. It fills the place of the Irish Juniper which is too tender here.

LITTLE GEM ARBOR VITAE—A very neat little dwarf, with fine foliage and compact, round head. Nice for the lawn—and cemetery.

WHITE PINE—This is without doubt one of the most valuable timber trees for the Northwest. It will do well on very light soils. It does not start as rapidly while young, but after ten years' planting is one of the fastest growers known. Fine for wind breakers.

MOUNTAIN PINE—A very dwarf species, compact. Foliage like the Scotch. Nice for lawn.

COLORADO BLUE SPRUCE—I quote from R. Douglas & Sons: "The Blue Spruce of Colorado, varies from dark green to light and dark blue in color. They are all beautiful, valuable and perfectly hardy, but the blue ones are the

most admired. Specimen trees of the Blue
Spruce, the Douglas Spruce of Colorado, and
the White Spruce, from 20 to 30 feet high, in
Massachusetts, Illinois, Iowa, Kansas and Nebraska, convince us that they will stand extreme
drouth in summer and extreme cold in winter
better than the common, so-called, hardy evergreens."

We have a few Blue Spruce, 2½ feet, extra
selected. Also the Douglas Spruce, 3 feet. They
will fill EARLIEST orders.

Deciduous Trees,

WHITE ASH—Needs no description. Is one
of the best trees for lawn or road line.

PURPLE-LEAVED BIRCH—With the habit of the
Birches, it has beautiful purple foliage. Very
desirable novelty.

CATALPA SPECIOSA—The hardy variety. A
very ornamental and valuable tree. Seems to
endure our worst winters.

AMERICAN LINDEN OR BASSWOOD—A rapid
growing, beautiful native tree, with very large
leaves and fragrant flowers. It is fine for lawn
or road-side.

AMERICAN WHITE ELM—The noble drooping
and spreading tree of our own woods. One of
the grandest of Park or street trees.

NORWAY MAPLE—A foreign variety with
large, broad leaves of a rich dark green. Probably the best maple in cultivation.

WIER'S CUT-LEAVED MAPLE—A Silver Maple
with remarkable and beautifully dissected foli-

age. Of rapid growth, shoots slender and drooping, giving it a graceful appearance. Should be in every collection.

BOLIEANA POPLAR—Lately introduced from Northern Russia. Does not sprout from the roots, is a very rapid grower, and is clean in habit. The leaves are almost black-green on the upper side and snow white underneath; when moved by the wind the trees present a most pleasing and unique appearance, distinct from all others. It is perfectly hardy.

CUT-LEAVED WEEPING BIRCH—An elegant, erect tree, with slender, drooping branches and fine cut leaves. A magnificent variety and worthy a place on every lawn.

OREL WEEPING WILLOW—From Orel, Russia. New here, but destined to become very popular, from its persistently weeping habit and extreme hardiness.

WISCONSIN WEEPING WILLOW—Of drooping habit and perfectly hardy.

Deciduous Shrubs.

TARTARIAN HONEY-SUCKLE—Perfectly hardy, both red and white varieties. Flowers in May.

HYDRANGEA GRANDIFLORA—A fine large semi-shrub, with showy panicles of white flowers in the greatest profusion. Is very nearly hardy here, but is better to be borne down and covered with evergreen boughs or something to hold the snow. Valuable for massing on the lawn.

DEUTZIA SCABRA — Rough-leaved; profuse flowering, white.

DEUTZIA GRACILIS—A charming species from Japan. Flowers pure white, and very delicate in bloom and foliage.

SPIREAS—Are all elegant, low shrubs of easiest culture and perfectly hardy. Billardi is rose-colored; Prunifolia, little white daisy like flowers; Douglasii, spikes of deep rose-colored flowers in July; Ulmifolia, large round clusters of white flowers; Lanceolata, lance-pointed foliage, and large, round clusters of white flowers that cover the whole plant; a charming shrub; Reevesii, flowers white and double, blooms freely in clusters. One of the best of the Spireas

SYRINGA PHILADELPHUS — A well-known shrub, with white, fragrant flowers.

ROSES.

NOTHING gives better satisfaction than a bed of Roses in the lawn. In a circular bed eight feet in diameter, 75 plants would be required of the ever blooming, and 50 of the Hybrid Perpetuals and Mosses. The effect is very fine, composed of the different colors in mass. Handfuls of bloom may be gathered daily from June till frost, on the bed of ever-blooming varieties. It is almost impossible to feed a rose too highly, nor is there danger of pruning too much.

CLIMBING ROSES.

PRAIRIE QUEEN —Clear, bright pink, compact and globular, and very double.

BALTIMORE BELLE – Pale blush, very double and great bloomer.

PRIDE OF WASHINGTON-- Brilliant amaranth, shaded rose center. Large clusters, very double and fine.

MOSS ROSES.

CAPT. INGRAM--Brilliant carmine, large full flowers, mossy buds.

PRINCESS ADELAIDE—One of the best. Extra large flowers, color bright rosy pink, very double and fragrant, beautifully mossed.

LUXEMBOURG — Bright crimson, large and double, very sweet and mossy.

MADAM DUPUY – White. Splendid large flowers, very double, sweet and mossy.

EVER-BLOOMING ROSES.

AURORA — Full, medium size, very double and sweet. Color silvery rose, beautifully shaded with clear pink.

ALICE SISLEY—A splendid rose. Large, very full and double, exceedingly sweet. Color a rare shade of violet red, brightened with crimson maroon. Elegant large pointed buds.

BELLA —Pure snow white, large size, very full and double. Tea scented. Splendid pointed buds.

ISABELLA SPRUNT -- Bright canary yellow, large beautiful buds, very sweet, tea scented, profuse bloomer.

PERLE DE LYON—Beautiful orange yellow with peach shading, sometimes coppery gold, stained with crimson. Charming buds and large, full flowers. Delicately perfumed.

HYBRID PERPETUAL ROSES.

BERNARD VARLET—A magnificent rose; large, full, globular form: color deep violet purple; free bloomer and very sweet.

ELIZA BOELOE—Very full and double, and delightfully perfumed. Color pure ivory white, sometimes clouded with blush and tinged with amber. Choice.

GEN. JACQUEMINOT — Rich velvety scarlet, changing to brilliant crimson. Magnificent buds.

PEONIE—One of the finest old roses. Never goes out of fashion. Not excelled by any. Very large, full flowers. Clear bright red, very sweet.

MAD. LOUIS CARRIQUE - Rich velvety crimson. Large size, very double, full and sweet.

Have described a few representatives of the different colors, among the hundreds of fine sorts.

TESTIMONIALS.

From Hon. Samuel Wade, of Paonia, Colo., Seventy-five miles west of Leadville, May 3, 1888.
Dear Sir:—The 100 Jessie strawberry plants came to hand on the 1st inst. all right and I have them well set. The plants were good ones and in excellent condition.

From J. Max Clark, one of the most active members of the original Greeley colonists, Colorado, Sept. 20, 1888.
"Friend Tuttle:—I have neglected to reply to your notice of shipment of Jessie plants, until I should be able to set them out and see how they turned out. There happened to be no water in the ditch when they arrived, and as they seemed in good condition, I thought they would do better in the package until I could get water than they would do set in the dry earth with what sprinkling I could give them, You will observe that we wait for water in this country instead of rain and it being very low and scarce at this time of the year, we have to take turns and wait until we can get it, I set them out yesterday morning, and as I got the ground moistened around them I think they will do well. [They were shipped in open basket, Sept. 18, therefore ten days in the package. A. C. T.]

From Otto Wasserzieher, Deerwood, Minn., Sept. 1st, 1888.
"Dear Sir:—The Jessie strawberry plants received in excellent condition, I think it a wonderful idea to send plants raised in pots, with lumps of dirt, picked in moss, because every plant is sure to grow."

From Hon. J. B. Dwinnell, Lodi, Columbia Co., Wis., Sept 20, 1888.
"Dear Sir:—The Jessie strawberry plants you sent me were received last Monday in fine order.

From H. H. Russell, Roslyn, Day Co., Dakota, Sept. 6, 1888.
Dear Sir:—The strawberry plants I got this morning and are planted, They were as fresh as if just taken out of their bed—could not be better.

From Mrs. J. S. Tripp, Prairie du Sac, Wis., Sept. 3, 1888.
"Dear Sir:—The strawberry plants arrived in prime condition. Not the least particle of earth was jarred from the roots. They were all, without exception, just as you removed them from the pots."

From N. F. Carpenter, Menominee, Wis Aug. 25, 1888
"Dear Sir:—The plants came through in No. 1 order."

From L. L. Inman, Havana, Steel County, Minn., Aug. 30, 1888
"Dear Sir:—The plants received all right. They were in nice shape. There are a number wanting plants, but I think they will now wait till next spring. Express charges $1

From E. W. Wagner, Lansing, Iowa, May 2, 1888.
"Dear Sir:—The trees arrived all right and am well pleased with them."

From Milo Barnard, afterward Pres. Ills. State Hort. Soc., Manteno, Ills., Apr. 30, 1888.
"Dear Sir:—The apple trees came to hand to-day in excellent condition. Accept thanks for high grade. etc.

From J. B. Ellison, Taylor Station, Jackson Co., Wis., May 9, 1888.
Dear Sir: "The trees and berry bushes were duly received. I am very much obliged for the extras; they were just what I wanted.

From Dr. Elliott Brown, of Fond du Lac, Wis., Sept. 20, 1888.
Dear Sir:—The potted Jessie strawberry plants came in good time and fine condition. They look thrifty and healthy, and should all grow. The packing was well done and I could see no reason why they should not cross the continent in perfect order. Thanks. Most all the things are budding out and I think they all will.

From Geo. Wright, of Wrightsville, Wis., May 23, 1888.
"Dear Sir:—I received the trees and plants in splendid order and was well satisfied. You have done more than well by me. I set them all out in a favorable time and they seem to be doing well."

From C. F. McNair, Nurseryman, Dansville, N. Y., Aug 29, 1887
The apple buds were received in good condition, were budded promptly and have made a fine catch.

From Chas. Luedloff, Carver Co., Minn., Nov. 12, 1887.
"Dear Sir:—The trees you sent came to hand in excellent condition, never got better trees, and packing was done in the best manner. Many thanks. Your business shall have my recommendation to my neighbors."

From John Pool, Avon, Ills., Sept, 17, 1887.
"Dear Sir:—Your retail price list at hand. I have noticed it some. I will send you a list of what I want and if you can send me as good stock as I received from you last year and at the same price, I will order. This was a hard year; the drouth has been so hard on trees set last spring, everybody is discouraged. Your trees stood the best of any in this country." October 25, Mr. Pool says, "My bill of trees came to hand to day in good shape and I am well pleased with the stock."

From M. S. Fawcett, of Lyon Co., Minn .
"Dear Sir—I would say that the small bill of trees and shrubs I got from you last fall has done very well. All the blackberries grew and are nice. But a few of the raspberries grew, the Fay currants are very nice. I nursed the Moore's Early Grape vine all summer and it finally sprouted about the first of August and is now growing finely. When I want more trees, etc., I will send to you."

Norway Spruce.